D0566631

This Boxer Books paperback belongs to

. . . .

www.boxerbooks.com

First Snow

For Olivia, my inspiration, and DB for believing in me.
B.F.

To Catherine.
S.B.

This paperback edition published in 2007
First published in Great Britain in 2005
by Boxer Books Limited
www.boxerbooks.com

Text copyright © 2005 Bernette Ford
Illustrations copyright © 2005 Sebastien Braun

The rights of Bernette Ford and Sebastien Braun to be identified
as the author and illustrator of this work have been asserted by them
in accordance with the Copyright, Designs and Patents Act, 1988.

All rights reserved, including the right of reproduction in whole or in part in any form.
A CIP catalogue record for this book is available from the British Library upon request.

ISBN 978-1-905417-14-8

1 3 5 7 9 10 8 6 4 2

Printed in China

First Snow

Written by Bernette Ford

Illustrated by Sebastien Braun

Boxer Books

It is dark —
a winter night.

The moon is bright,
barely there behind
a lazy haze of grey.

Snow begins to fall — first slowly —
big flakes softly falling, melting fast.

Then, falling faster —
swirling, blowing, twirling down
to cover up the meadow.

Far below the cold white blanket,
Bunny and his sisters and brothers
nestle closer to their mother,
keeping each other warm
and dreaming of green grass
on the meadow.

Suddenly, Bunny awakes from his nap —
slowly, softly creeps out of his warm lair.

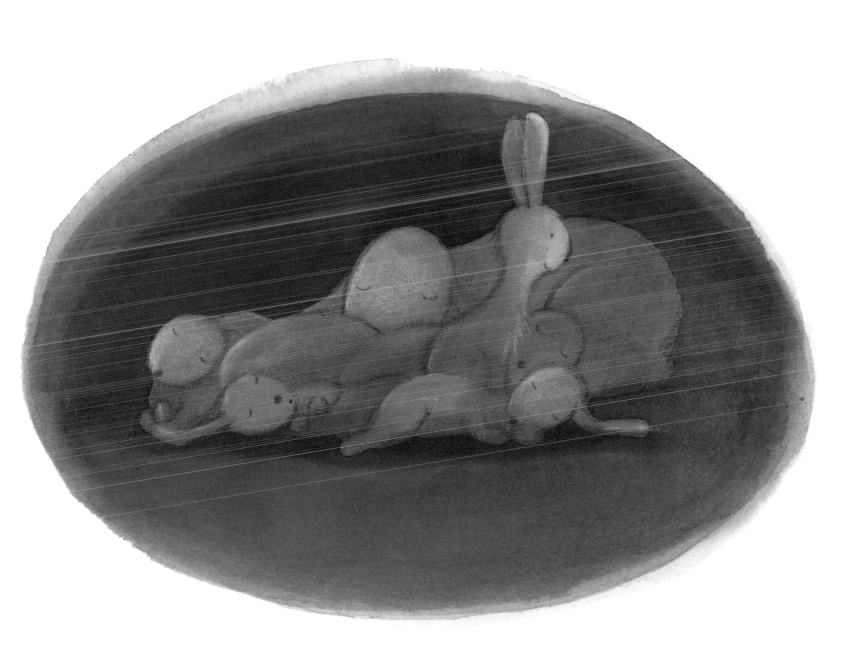

Up pokes his small nose
to sniff the air.
It is cold for early winter.

Brothers and sisters
follow Bunny out
into the cold first snow.

Soon the whistling winds die down
and it is quiet in the meadow.

Curious bunnies, always listening,
hop across the glistening meadow.

Seeing shadows on the meadow,
bunnies hide to watch the night-time.

Bunnies see the hungry chipmunks
snooping under drooping branches . . .

scurrying to gather pine cones
in the cold first snow.

There a grey wolf
on the prowl.
There a barn owl,
swooping down
to search for dinner.
Bunnies know to
keep on hiding
in the cold
first snow.

Soon there's moonlight on the meadow.
Soon the houses glow with lamplight.
Smoke and smells curl up and out
of all the chimneys.

Children bundled up against the wind
come out to play in the cold first snow.

Now bunnies race across the meadow,
leaving paw prints as they go.

Hopping . . .

stumbling . . .

rolling . . .

tumbling . . .

playing in the cold first snow!

Bunnies stop to watch the children
as they hurry home for cocoa —
cheeks and noses all aglow.

Children leave a fat white snowman
gleaming in the bright white moonlight —

beaming at the bunnies in the cold first snow.

Other Boxer Books paperbacks

The Lost Ears: **Phillida Gili**

Once upon a time there lived a teddy called
Harry, who was only two and a half inches tall.
Then one day something completely unexpected
happened to him. . .
ISBN13: 978-1-905417-44-5

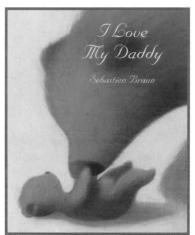

I Love My Daddy: **Sebastien Braun**

Sometimes parents are loud and playful.
Sometimes they are quiet and compassionate.
And they are always loving.
Shortlisted - Best New Illustrator 2006
BOOKTRUST EARLY YEARS AWARDS
ISBN13: 978-0-954737-39-9

Big Smelly Bear: **Britta Teckentrup**

Big Smelly Bear never washed, brushed or took a bath.
Big Smelly Bear was followed by a big smelly stink
wherever he went.
Until one day when he met a new friend.
Could she persuade Big Smelly Bear to take a bath?
ISBN13: 978-1-905417-43-8